Life's Winding

(The Sequel to Perseverance Road)

B

R

O

T

H

E

R

S

JOSEPHINE (JO) LA RUSSA GRAVEN

ISBN 978-1-954693-55-5

FV-5

www.IntellectPublishing.com

intellect Publishing ™

Acknowledgement

This book is dedicated to the many individuals who read my published book, **Perseverance Road,** and encouraged me to write the sequel. You wanted to know more about the Cole family, the tunnel construction, and the continuation of the Cole family lives. Readers, may your curiosity be satisfied with the intertwined lives of sons and parents as the responsibility of the parents is shifted to the two sons, Peter and Allen.

I am eternally grateful to my middle daughter, Dawn Graven Brown, who asked to edit my writing and made suggestions for correctness and clarity. Thank you, Dawn.

Love Mom

Prologue

Life's Winding Road is the sequel to **Perseverance Road** which was published March, 2021. Perseverance Road main characters are Tom and Flora Cole. Their overspending and unemployment caused numerous hardships. They had to move from city life in West Virginia to a deserted cabin in Appalachia's hills of Kentucky. Tom started all over in the new career of lumbering, then road construction. Flora became a crafter and used that hobby for income.

I ended that book with the hint of possible danger of the tunnel construction. This sequel shares the lives of their two sons, Peter and Allen, as they enter adulthood.

In **Life's Winding Road**, the story continues with the tunnel construction dialog. The Cole brothers have completed high school and begin journeying down the twists and turns of adulthood as their lives evolve. Both have different means to enter and pay for college. While in college, they both change majors and the curves provided new more promising futures. As children and as teenagers their parents were the providers. In the sequel, those roles are reversed and the sons take the responsibility for their parents' care. The end may surprise you and possibly lead to yet another sequel.

What roads in life will each travel to create new possibilities for their future? What happens to the parents that necessitates the sons help? Peter's girlfriend says No to his marriage proposal after they have dated for five years? Why? You will never know until you turn the pages of this book.

Life's Winding Road is fiction. All the characters, events and locations in this book are figments of my imagination.

Table of Contents

Life's Winding Road

(The Sequel to Perseverance Road)

JOSEPHINE (JO) LA RUSSA GRAVEN

Disturbing News

Mike McCord gave his construction team a $100.00 bonus when the mountain parkway was completed in mid-May after two years of clearing the land and constructing the 120 miles of the mountain parkway. He told his construction team that Wheeler Explosive Company had been hired to do the initial blasting of the tunnel between Kentucky and West Virginia. Albert Wheeler, the owner of the explosive company, told Mike McCord the first phase of blasting would begin around, June 5th. McCord told his men to enjoy the next two weeks before returning to work and removing blasted rock.

Albert Wheeler had to have a federal inspection of the type of rock to be blasted and found it was quartzite, an extremely hard rock. Blasting of this type of rock would require a new boring machine to cut through the mile of rock. There were only four of these machines in America and all four were in operation on other projects in various cities across the country. It would be late June or early July before one of the massive machines could be transported to the tunnel site. Wheeler's company would do one blasting at the entrance of the tunnel in Kentucky and another blasting at the exact location on the West Virginia side of the tunnel. The two had to be identical.

McCord didn't have another project and had to lay his workers off. Allen Cole was depending on working that summer for McCord just as he had the previous two summers. The money earned would be added to his savings to cover college expenses, if he got an art scholarship when graduating in May as Mr. Willard, his high school art teacher, thought he would.

There were only 46 students who had stayed in school and were graduating. Many of the boys quit school when they turned sixteen and went to work in the coal mines or lied about their age and enlisted in the military. Some were serving in the Korean War. Both were ways to send money home to their families to ease the poverty. Neither of the McCord sons graduated. Jeb went in the military and was learning to be an airplane mechanic. Ted quit school and worked with his dad.

As Allen sat in the school auditorium on graduation night, his mind kept drifting to other possibilities if he didn't get a scholarship. He had worked for Mr. McCord on and off for the past two years. He'd saved most of his earnings, but was it enough to pay for expenses not covered by an award? What college? Where? He wondered of the cost of books, art supplies, fees, gas for his car, and a little spending money. If he calculated correctly and got to work every single day for eight weeks, he'd make $374.40.

Peter, Allen's older brother, could not attend graduation. He was taking his finals at Blyne College where he attended. His high school counselor had helped him get a full scholarship from his high school in West Virginia to study forestry. Allen was graduating from a school in Kentucky that he had attended during his junior and senior years. Art was his talent and few colleges gave awards in the arts.

A minister gave the invocation, followed by the student body president's speech. Finally, the principal and acting counselor stood. The principal congratulated the students who had completed their education, then the counselor began calling the students to the stage to receive their diploma. No mention was made of scholarships. Allen felt his dream of a college scholarship was not happening. He looked down at his clashed hands and his mind drifted to other possibilities of earning enough to pay for college. He thought of the military as an option. If he didn't get a scholarship, how long would he have to work to save that much money? Where would he go to college? Would he major in art? Could he make a good living as an artist? So many questions to consider.

Allen's name was called and he walked across the stage to Mr. Rogers, the principal. Mr. Rogers put his hand on Allen's shoulder and announced that he had received a partial scholarship to the University of Cincinnati. The audience capped and his parents beamed.

The award was sealed in an envelope that he was handed along with his diploma. His spirits lifted and he smiled as the audience applauded. His parents looked over his shoulder as he opened and read the letter. It stated he was awarded a four-year partial scholarship. The letter did not state what a partial scholarship would pay. It ended with an invitation to visit the school and learn what expenses would be covered.

Allen's girlfriend, Alecia, received a full scholarship from the Atlanta School of Art. Her dad whistled, then yelled, "That's my girl!" Allen gave her a thumbs up, stood and clapped until she returned to her seat. He was happy for her, but disappointed. They had hoped to both get art scholarships at the same school. Atlanta was seven hours away. They wouldn't see each other except at Christmas break and during the summer.

Tough Decision

Allen's parents said they would give him some money to pay his expenses not covered by the award from their savings. Tom Cole was earning $3,300.00 a year. They didn't owe anything. If they gave him the difference for college, they wouldn't have much left to save. He couldn't accept that much money. His dad's foot bothered him more each day. How long would he be able to work? Yes, his mother earned some money from her crafts, but was it fair to deprive her of her earnings? He thought he could make frames for some of his sketches of the men toiling over the tobacco during harvest or frame some of his bird pictures and send them to Hoppersville with his mother. Could he earn enough? He decided he couldn't ask them to sacrifice everything for him. He had to find his own way.

On Monday morning after graduation, Allen wrote a letter to the college. He asked how much his award would pay each semester and what cost would he have to cover. A reply letter came two weeks later. The letter stated $400.00 of his cost per semester would be covered. He would have a $50.00 per semester credit at the college bookstore for books. He would be responsible for the

$380.00 per semester room and board, library fee of $10.00 each semester, and any miscellaneous fees or supplies.

On June 5th, Albert Wheeler told Mike McCord the federal inspection of the tunnel site would be at least another week before a team could come to the site. They would have to sample the rock to determine the best way to blast out the near mile of rock.

McCord was frustrated as he didn't know how long they would be without work.

To Tom and Flora, the lay-off seemed like a repeat of the "pink slip" of the coal strip mining job some years before and the loss of their house. At least now they had no debt and they owned outright the cabin and land, but where did that leave Allen and his hope of college?

Allen thought seriously about his parents' problem and how, not having a more stable future, changed their lives. He wondered will it happen again?

Allen's mind was constantly thinking of other possibilities to earn money. He had heard that many of the communities had festivals to sell their crafts. He had art pads full of pictures. Could he frame them and travel to the different communities to sell his drawings? Would they sell and at what price? He went to the Laneville festival with eight framed pictures. Only two sold. He made eight dollars that day and quickly he realized that was not the answer.

The following Monday, he gassed up his car and told his parents he was going to the college to see if they had other means for him to pay for college. The college was seventy-nine miles from home. He told his parents he would stay two days at the YMCA. His mother packed him a lunch and snacks to ease the expense. His dad gave him five dollars to ensure he had enough for food and gas. He bought a map of Cincinnati for fifteen cents. He located the college and went to the registrar's office. Allen showed the representative the scholarship letter he was awarded. Allen inquired who he needed to talk to about financial help. The young woman told him there were financial options and directed him to the Financial Aid Office. Again, he shared the scholarship letter, explained his parents could not pay for his college expenses, and asked what financial help could this office arrange? He asked, were there jobs on campus that he could do?

The financial advisor told Allen, "There is a job sweeping the auditorium Monday through Friday and after special events. It doesn't pay money; however, it would cover $100.00 of your semester expense. The advisor explained that job couldn't be awarded until Allen had enrolled. If you live on campus, you could work in the cafeteria serving meals or cleaning-up. You would work at two of the three meals each day and would receive three meals a day in exchange for your work. There again, you must be enrolled in the college and must live on campus."

The advisor shared financial aid packets. "You would have to apply for a loan each semester, but would not start payments on those loans until after you graduate."

That option reminded Allen of the money problems his parents had and the loss of their home. He wasn't interested in borrowing large sums of money over a four-year span of college. He asked again, "Is there any way I could pay for my college

The advisor said, "You could co-op. If you choose to co-op, you would attend classes one semester and work for a company in your field of study the next semester. It would take you six years to graduate, but you would have no debt when you graduate ver, I don't know of a museum or art gallery that accepts co-op students."

Allen thanked the advisor, collected the material he'd shared and left. None of the options sounded good to him. He ate at White Castle. For $1.10, he had five roll-size hamburgers and a glass of water. He thought, 'this would be a luxury if I don't have any other income.' Allen checked in at the YMCA and said he'd be staying two nights. From his window, he could see the National Guard Recruiting Office across the street. He stared at the building for a long time and wondered it that was the answer to his dilemma. He didn't sleep well. He tossed and turned and kept waking up. He kept thinking about joining the National Guard as an option. He'd have training and a monthly weekend of duty with pay. Was this the answer?

The next morning, he ate the apple and some of the cookies his mother had packed. He got a free cup of black coffee at the entrance to the YMCA and walked outside. He sipped his coffee and stared at the recruiting center and pondered if he should join. He walked across the street and opened the door as the bells of a church rang eight times.

The aged recruiter looked-up, then got up from his desk and put out his hand to Allen and said, "Good morning, are you here to join the National Guard?"

Allen was apprehensive about how eager the recruiter seemed. He replied, "I'm here to learn more about the National Guard before I make a decision."

The recruiter said, "Have a seat and let's share. Would you like a cup of coffee?" as he poured one for himself.

Allen shook his head to indicate 'no'.

The recruiter took a sip of his coffee and said, "Tell me about yourself and why you are considering joining the National Guard."

Allen shared, "I recently graduated from high school and I was awarded a partial art scholarship to the University of Cincinnati. I had planned to work on a road construction project as I have done for the last two summers, but federal regulations and inspections have delayed the start of that phase of construction until mid-July or later. The explosive company will not blast its way through the mountain, but will use a boring machine to grind out the rock. There is a question as to when the machine can be transported to the site."

"I spoke with the college financial advisor. I was told my award would pay the tuition each semester and provide a $50.00 book credit at the college bookstore. It doesn't cover room or board, incidental fees or art supplies."

Allen waited for the recruiting officer to reply. He had a pencil in his hand and was twirling it back and forth, but said nothing for a few minutes.

He asked Allen, "What do you know about the guard? Are you familiar with the function, the training and the possibility of deploying if there is a national disaster? There is a war in Korea. If needed, guard units could be deployed to a war zone. What do you think about that possibility?"

Allen responded, "I know there is training, once a month duty ,and summer training. I know there is pay for all these components, but not how much. If I sign up today, will I have time to do my training this summer and hopefully, earn enough to start college in the fall?"

"You are basically correct; however, joining the National Guard is more than that. As a part of the enlisting process, you will begin with a physical. If you pass it, you will be given immunization shots, issued a uniform, have your hair shaved, and be shipped to a military base for ten weeks of rigorous physical training, the same as any soldier in any branch of the military. Yes, you will serve one weekend a month. The unit assigned will determine what specialty you will learn. If there is a national emergency, such as a hurricane disaster, your unit might be called into duty to assist. There is a war right now. On rare occasion, guard units are sent. Yes, you will receive pay."

Allen asked, "How much would I be paid for the ten weeks of training, for the monthly duty and for the two weeks of summer maneuver training? If I join, when will the next boot camp begin and where?"

The officer said, "There are two boot camps scheduled for this summer. Fort Loftin in Wheaten, Kansas, will leave this Monday, on June 13 and the second scheduled boot camp will be at Fort Reeves outside of Sumpter, South Carolina and scheduled to leave on Thursday, June 19. You asked about pay. As a new recruit, you will earn $75.00/month or $180.00 for boot camp. Monthly weekend duty pay is $25.00. For the two weeks after your initial year of service, pay is $100.00. As you are promoted in rank, your pay would increase."

"Son, you could also cut your cost if you rented a room in a private home. Some even provide meals. There are plenty of older people who live near the college in those big houses. The older people could use the extra income and like having someone living in the house with them. You seem unsure as to what to do. Go home, talk to your dad, look at all your options, and if you decide on the National Guard, I'll be right here with the paperwork for you to enlist."

He shook the recruiter's hand and left. He bought a newspaper and looked in the classified section. There were rooms advertised for college students attending the University of Cincinnati. Allen walked the mile to the college and looked for the streets with rooms advertised. Most were listed for twenty dollars/month. One or two offered a breakfast as a part of the rent. He found a couple of apartments for twenty-five dollars/month. They were small with space heaters, small old refrigerator and two-burner gas stove. If he rented one of these apartments in the fall and brought fruits and vegetables his mother canned, and joined the National Guard, he could make it.

Allen contemplated all that he had learned in the past two days as he drove home. He saw his mother in her garden and his dad raking the yard as he parked his car. His dad met him as he walked toward the cabin. His dad asked if he'd found a job that would pay for the difference in expenses after the scholarship. Allen shook his head to indicate no. He asked his dad if they could go for a walk. They walked in the wooded area around the property, then sat by the pond and Allen told his dad of all the possibilities to earn the money needed. Then he turned to his dad and asked, "What should I do?"

His dad faced his son and replied, "That is a decision only you can make, son."

A Change in Majors

Near the end of Peter's spring semester of his sophomore year, he had a meeting with his advisor. Peter explained he was switching majors from forestry to pre-med. His advisor asked why he was making such a drastic change.

Peter told his advisor of Mr. Cleburne's offer to pay for him to become a veterinarian and in exchange, he promised to work as Mr. Cleburne's veterinarian for at least ten years.

"Pre-Med," the advisor said, "is one of the hardest majors Blyne College offers. You have completed most of your required basic classes, and that is good. Your final two years or more of pre-med will be intense and require long labs each week for each science class Most require a two or three-hour lab every week. You will have to take an upper-level biology class and chemistry class each semester plus a higher-level math and/or statistic class. Can you handle that and work thirty hours a week for Mr. Cleburne? Let's look at your new course and decide what would be best for you to take this summer. An Understanding of Scientific Terminology would be a book I recommend you buy. It will be an invaluable resource that you can refer to often. There is a one-hour course called etymology that references the origin or meaning of word parts and how they work together. I suggest you take etymology, anatomy, a three-hour class, and biochemistry, a three-hour class. Both anatomy and biochemistry have a weekly three-hour lab. Both deal with the functions of the body. Anatomy teaches you about the body parts and their location. Biochemistry teaches how your body use its body parts and how the two work together. It will also make physiology in the fall semester easier. I know seven hours in summer session is considered an overload, but you will find the etymology class is an easy course. Can you handle the recommended seven hours this summer and a thirty-hour work week for Mr. Cleburne?"

Peter replied, "I intend to take the overload and rearrange my work schedule."

Peter left the advisor's office and went to the college bookstore. First, he looked through the used books to see if there was an etymology book, a scientific terminology book, and an anatomy book or a biochemistry book.

He found an etymology book that looked brand new. There was a used anatomy book with underlining on most chapters. He asked for a new copy of the scientific terminology book. The biochemistry book was out of stock, but the shipment was due the next week. The clerk wrote the books he brought to her on his account that would be paid by Mr. Cleburne. The clerk smiled as she handed him his bag of books and told Peter to enjoy his reading.

Peter thanked her and went to one of the empty living rooms at Yocum House. He spent the rest of the afternoon reading from the etymology book. He had planned to go home for the four days he had off, but decided to go home on Saturday and come back Sunday after lunch instead.

As usual, his mother fixed all his favorite foods. It rained both days and he sat on the porch with his anatomy book. He read all the underlined material. He felt he knew much of the content from high school biology and from working with the horses. It made him aware of how similar animals and humans are.

Peter had etymology one day a week as a morning class followed by biochemistry on Tuesday and Thursday. He had anatomy on Monday, Wednesday and Friday followed by the three-hour lab on Wednesday. He had completed his biochemistry lab by lunchtime on Thursday then went to the farm until six o'clock. Seven-hours of class and six hours weekly in lab, plus working with the horses at odd hours on the farm, left him little time to do anything else. His one-hour nightly dates with Maria were all the free time he had.

Peter was thankful he'd been advised to take etymology and to purchase a scientific terminology book as a reference source. He referred to them often.

The brothers stayed up late and talked. Allen shared his dilemma. He hoped he'd made the right decisions. Peter listened, but like their dad, felt only Allen could decide what he was going to do. Peter shared his change in major.

Peter wrote a postcard to his parents every other week. He was extremely busy and spending most of his free time studying. He apologized that he wouldn't come home before the end of August for maybe a week, but he was looking forward to his momma's good cooking. With each postcard, he asked about his dad's foot, but his dad never replied about the pain he was experiencing. He had a lot of science classes to take. He shared he wouldn't be able to apply for veterinarian school until he'd graduated in pre-med and had worked one hundred-fifty hours in some phase of animal care. He hoped his work with Mr. Cleburne's racehorses would count.

Veterinarian School is ten straight semesters, no summer breaks. The University of Kentucky has three dates for enrollment and classes-January, June and September. Peter seemed perplexed. He ran his hand through his hair, looked at his brother and said, "I've bought an engagement ring for Maria and had hopes of asking her to marry me when I finished pre-med, but now there is one-hundred fifty hours of work before I can even be considered for vet school. I don't know if she will wait five years for marriage."

Allen asked his brother, "Have you and Maria talked about marriage? You have dated a long time. Is she as in love as you are?"

Peter was shocked that Allen asked if Maria was in love with him.

The Brothers

After Peter finished finals in June at the completion of his sophomore year of college and before the summer session began, he went home for a couple of days. He had not been home since Christmas. Peter missed the family being together, sharing meals and spending time with his brother, Allen. His mother had written him that Allen had a partial scholarship to the University of Cincinnati. She shared that the mountain tunnel project would have a delayed start due to some government regulations and the arrival of a big machine for excavating the rock from the mountain that was intended to be safer. Of course, this meant a temporary lay-off. If Allen got to work for McCord, it would possibly be six weeks, not twelve weeks. There wasn't a guarantee that phase of the tunnel would begin by even July first. Peter felt he needed to go home. He had an uneasy feeling about the tunnel construction.

Peter had difficult courses of study, mostly biology and chemistry classes. His advisor suggested he take seven hours in summer school. He needed a good background in medical terminology. The advisor recommended he take a chemistry and related biology class during the summer sessions. She advised him to buy the books for these courses and begin reading them immediately. There would be a lot of memorizations with a change from forestry to pre-med.

Peter got home mid-morning and found his mother in her garden, his dad on the porch whittling, and his younger brother on a picnic with his girlfriend. He sat on the porch swing, and he and his dad enjoyed the quiet of this homesite. His momma had not heard the truck engine nor seen him pull into the yard. As she pulled her wagon of vegetables to the cabin, she saw him, dropped the handle of the wagon and ran to him with open arms. He stood and waited for her. His dad smiled at seeing his wife and son hug. His mother pulled back from Peter and noticed how much he had changed in the past six months.

Peter brought the wagon of vegetables to the cabin for his mother as she brought out a dish of cookies. As they munched on the cookies, he told them it would take years to complete a pre-med degree, then there would be ten straight semesters to complete veterinarian school. To get into vet school, he had to complete one-hundred-fifty hours of on-the-job training. He hoped his working with the racehorses could be counted for the one hundred-fifty hours.

As the parents and Peter sat down to eat supper that evening, Allen charged in the front door with the empty picnic basket. He dropped it by the door and seated himself as the family reached for hands to say the blessing.

It pleased Flora and Tom to have their sons at home for a meal and a few days visit. The brothers sent their parents to the sofa to listen to the baseball game on the radio as they cleaned the kitchen.

Peter and Allen went out on the porch and talked late into the night. Allen shared what he had found out about his scholarship and the potentials for funding to pay the rest of the cost. He told his brother the financial aid advisor mentioned the possibility of a job sweeping the auditorium with one hundred dollars being applied to the cost not covered by the award. He could work in the college cafeteria in exchange for his meals. Allen told Peter he wouldn't be able to apply for either until he had enrolled and was living on campus. Allen saw both of those jobs as maybe, not assured jobs. Allen said the third option the advisor mentioned was student loans which he'd have to apply for each semester. Student loans were payable after graduation. The student loans with payments after graduating, reminded Allen of the family losing the house because of the prolong lay-off and family debts. He wanted no part of a large debt to be paid over years after graduation.

Allen told Peter, when he went to Cincinnati to find out about his scholarship, he stayed for two days at the YMCA. It gave him time to look over the campus, look for a possible job, and visit the various buildings and sites. From his YMCA window he could see the National Guard

Recruiting office across the street. He wondered if that a way to finance his schooling?

Allen said, "The next morning, I decided to visit the recruiting office. I ate the apple and cookies momma had packed for me and drank a cup of coffee before I walked into the recruiter's office. The recruiter asked if I was there to enlist and I told him I wanted to find out more about the National Guard."

Allen continued, "The recruiter explained the enlistment/rigorous boot camp with duty once a month and two weeks of summer training each year. The older officer reminded me of the pay as he handed me a pen and some papers to sign. I just sat there. I was undecided. I needed time to look at all the options before I made that kind of decision."

He pulled the enlistment form back and said, "Think about the guard. If it is the right decision for you, come back to see me."

"After I got home, I told dad all I'd learned and asked for his guidance. He said, I had to make that decision."

"I've thought about it all week and I've decided to join the Guard. National Guard pay will cover the difference for college expenses and my scholarship. If Mr. McCord has work for me next summer, or thereafter, it would give me more money. Basic training begins in a week, so I am going to join on Thursday."

Peter listened to his brother, but felt Allen had to make that decision. Peter explained there are many steps he must accomplish before getting into vet school including work experience. He named off some of the required classes, anatomy, physiology, biochemistry, bacteriology, genetics, organic and inorganic chemistry, quantitative and qualitative analysis, and advanced math classes

Peter seemed perplexed. He ran his hand through his hair, looked at his brother and said , "I've bought an engagement ring for Maria and had hopes of asking her to marry me when I finish pre-med, but now there is one hundred-fifth hours of work before I can even be considered for vet school. I don't know if she will wait five years for marriage."

Allen listened to his brother then asked, "Have you and Maria discussed getting married? Is she as eager as you to get married while you are still in school?"

Peter didn't respond to his brothers questioning.

Allen Enlists

Monday morning at breakfast, Allen told his parents he was going back to Cincinnati to join the National Guard. It would give him the money needed to pay for college. Once he signed the enlistment papers, he would stay in Cincinnati for the week before boot camp. He would have his physical to make sure he qualified then he would check into the YMCA for the remainder of time until the new recruits would be picked up at the Cincinnati office and transported to boot camp in Sumpter, South Carolina on Thursday.

His mother's body language and the tears swelling in her eyes indicated her concern for his decision, but she said nothing. She knew he had been deep in thought all the past week, wrestling with what to do. He packed a few items to take with him. He shook hands with his dad and gave his mother a hug, then climbed in his car and waved as he pulled out of the dirt driveway.

He drove to his girlfriend, Alecia's home and picked her up. They drove to the creek near the church and had a picnic lunch. He looked at the smile on her face and wished they could be closer when attending college, but that was an impossible dream. He pulled her close and kissed her, then took her hand and walked along the wooded path beside the creek. They removed their shoes and ran through the cool water laughing. They climbed up on a boulder and he told her he was joining the National Guard. It would provide enough money to pay expenses not covered by his partial scholarship. They sat there and held hands Allen told her he'd be leaving for Cincinnati after he took her home. He put his arm around her shoulder, and they sat there in silence for a period of time, then slowly walked back to his car. He drove her home, gave her a kiss and said he'd write to her when he could. She promised to write to him and would spend time with him during Christmas break.

Allen was somber as he drove back the seventy-nine miles back to Cincinnati. He kept second guessing himself. Had he made the right decision? He didn't hesitate when he got to the recruiting center. He walked in and was greeted by the same recruiter. Allen told him he was ready to join. A stack of enlistment papers was handed to Allen. Each page was explained before Allen signed.

The college was less than a mile from the YMCA and he walked around the college He stopped by the administration office and asked if it was possible for him to see the dorm assigned to freshmen boys? Could he pay for a meal in the cafeteria and could he stroll through the buildings where classes were held? He was told he could walk the campus and see the location of all the facilities. He was given a map and told, if he came back the next morning at nine a.m. to the registrar office, there would be someone to give him a guided tour. He ate supper at the White Castle Restaurant. He ate five roll-sized hamburgers, had a soda and a slice of chocolate cream pie.

His car was parked in front of the YMCA, and he realized he had to make arrangements to get it back home. It could not sit in front of the YMCA for ten weeks. He didn't even know if the new recruits would come back to this city or be released in Sumpter, South Carolina where they were going for boot camp. There was a pay phone near the campus. He dropped the fifteen cents in the phone, then called the McCord's home. He asked Mrs. McCord, if she would go to his parents' cabin and give his parents a message?

She said, "Yes"

Allen said, "I can't keep my car here for ten weeks. I need to get it home. Could you ask my parents to meet me at the front entrance of the Cincinnati Zoo Wednesday around 10 a.m.?" Allen continued, "It cost a dollar admission per person at the zoo and I will buy the tickets. We can spend a few hours together."

Mrs. McCord drove over to the Cole's cabin and relayed Allen's message. Flora was just taking two loaves of cinnamon bread out of the oven. The aroma of baked bread and the cinnamon smelled so good. Flora asked her if she had a few minutes to have a slice with butter and honey. Emmy McCord could not resist. She sat at the table and ate the hot bread oozing with honey as Flora told her of Allen's plans to serve in the National Guard. It would provide the money he needed for schooling and maybe another job opportunity. Flora took the half-eaten loaf of bread and wrapped it up. She handed it to Emmy McCord and said, "You and Mike enjoy it for breakfast. "

Tom and Flora stood on the porch and watched as their neighbor drove out of their yard. Tom turned toward his wife and said, "It's time we get a telephone. Our sons are too far away to visit often or for us to visit. The eight dollars a month for a telephone will be well spent."

Tuesday afternoon, Tom filled the gas tank, checked the fluid levels in Flora's car, checked the tire pressure, and made sure all the belts were secure. He bought a map of the state of Kentucky and Ohio. Cincinnati was located just inside the state line of Ohio. He checked the roads they would travel to determine what time they needed to leave the next morning. Flora would drive her car back home and Tom would drive Allen's car. The distance would take at least two and one-half hours driving time each way. He determined they needed to leave by seven a.m. Wednesday morning. There weren't any freeways in the small cities between their home place and Cincinnati. As they crossed the Ohio River into Ohio, they saw the sign for the Cincinnati Zoo It was one-and-a-half miles ahead.

Allen was waiting for his parents at the front gate. He waved to them as they turned into the near empty parking lot. He watched them as they walked toward him. His dad holding his mother's hand. His mother had a bag in her hand. He smiled. He knew she had brought something she had made to eat at lunch.

He had already purchased the tickets and handed them to the ticket taker as they walked through the gate. For two hours, they walked around the zoo. None of them had ever been to a zoo. They marveled at the number and variety of animals from all parts of the world. There was constant chatter from different animals. They couldn't believe that so many monkeys could be housed in such a small, fenced cage. They laughed at their playfulness as they swung from bar to bar. They were amazed at the height of the giraffe and to read from the zoo brochure that no two are identical. The giraffe, it said, has no voice that can be heard and because of the distance from its head to rest of its body it has two circulatory systems. There was a newborn giraffe that was already five feet tall. It was just getting enough strength in its legs to stand, but kept falling down again. The sign in front of the cage said, "Help name the baby giraffe. Put your suggestion in this box."

They watched as the polar bear splashed in the water to cool off. Flora grabbed Tom's arm as they went around a bend in a path and heard the roar of a lion. Tom and

Allen laughter as she realized it was a lion in an enclosed area, not on the loose coming around the bend. Once she realized there was no danger, she laughed too.

They heard the songsters in a different area and could not believe the vivid colors, sizes and voices. They ended their visit at the zoo watching a program of a zookeeper talking about falcons. He had a huge bird on a leather strap that was perched on his steel mesh gloved hand. He let it fly over the heads of those seated. Everyone in its path ducked. He whistled, and the bird returned to hm.

They sat at a picnic table near the entrance, bought bottled water and ate lunch. Allen's momma had ham and cheese slices packed in ice, a jar of applesauce and the cinnamon bread she had made the day before. She had a brown paper bag with a dozen molasses cookies that she had stored in her cookie jar. They held hands and said a blessing. As they ate, his parents asked if the college was near and could they see the campus. His parents climbed in his car and he took them to see the college. They walked the quadrangle and he pointed out the dorm where he would live, the cafeteria, the library, and the buildings for classes. He said there was a chapel on the far end of campus where he'd probably attend services. He seemed so excited. They left the campus and he drove back to the zoo parking lot. It was time to leave, and Allen handed his dad his car keys. His Mother handed him the brown bag with the remainder of molasses cookies and cinnamon bread. She told him to take care of himself as she gave him a long hug. He watched as they drove away. He had a feeling of emptiness as he stood there all alone. Allen paid a nickel and rode the bus back to the YMCA.

Boot Camp

There were seventeen young men in front of the recruiting office at 0600 hours Thursday morning when the white bus with National Guard painted on the side arrived. An officer in fatigues climbed out of the bus to welcome them. A storage bin was opened, and they put their belongings in, then climbed in the bus. They were offered black coffee and donuts as they began their journey. The bus traveled through large cities with heavy traffic, then open areas with fields and farm homes, over mountains and finally a major highway. They rode down Highway 77 toward Charlotte, North Carolina by the time Allen drifted off to sleep. Others slept as they traveled east then south to South Carolina The bus only stopped twice that day for lunch and for supper. It was midnight when the sergeant on board told them they were at their destination. They were taken to their barracks with rows of single cots. Each had a pillow, a set of sheets and pillowcase on top. They made their beds and crawled in them.

At 0500 hours the next morning, reveille was played. The young men jumped out of their beds, put on the fatigues that were handed to them and told to assemble outside for a morning run.

The drill sergeant said, "Since you guys just got here last night, we will only do a five-mile run before mess."

He moved to the side of the first row and began to run. At first, it was flat ground, then hills. The drill sergeant barked, "Stay in line boys. Before you know it, you will be running ten miles each morning. Take a shower and be in the mess hall in fifteen minutes, if you want chow."

The new recruits howled when they realized the showers only had cold water. There was no privacy. One wall was shower heads. Toilets and urinals were also in the open. They had not expected such openness. They went through the line and got their trays and set in an assigned area. Starved after their morning run, they gobbled down their food and washed it down with strong black coffee. They spent the rest of the morning getting their heads shaved, getting immunization shots, picking up more fatigues and equipment.

After lunch, the young men gathered in a large hall with other new recruits from other areas. They learned base rules and procedures. They were told that every morning, they would have at least a five-mile run, and they would have field training, artillery training, aggression maneuvers, and much more. They were to follow all orders. Allen and many others had not expected this much rigidity.

Allen called home twice during boot camp and told his mother not to worry about him. He was fine. He told his momma he was learning a lot and meeting guys from all over the United States. When his dad got on the phone, he told him how tough the training was. He told his dad, "When I return home, I'll be a man, a soldier."

Allen kept telling himself he could handle whatever they required. It meant he would get his college degree. He counted off the weeks, and realized how he had grown physically and mentally. His chest had expanded, and his muscles were bulging. He stood erect, became more observant, and responded quickly to happenings in his surroundings. He knew he was no longer a boy. He was a citizen soldier.

At the end of the ten weeks, a ceremony was held, and parents were invited, but few could afford to come. The new guardsmen were paid for their training and released to go home. It took two days for the Trailways Bus to get to the stop near his home. The bus stopped at every town to let passengers off or to pick up more travelers.

Allen stopped at the mercantile store and bought some butterscotch hard candy, then he walked up the mountain to the cabin. His parents weren't home. He put his duffle bag in his room. He went into the kitchen, opened his mother's cookie jar and got a handful of sugar cookies and munched them as he searched the refrigerator for something more substantial to eat. He grabbed a plate of cold fried chicken and a glass of lemonade, then he went on the porch to wait for his parents.

Allen's parents were talking as they drove into the yard, and did not notice him sitting on the porch. He got up and walked out to his dad's truck and opened the door for his Momma. She sat there with her mouth open then jumped out of the truck and gave her son a big hug. He had a smile on his face as he leaned down and kissed her on her forehead. His Dad was chuckling as he limped around his truck to give his son a hug.

Dorm Life

Allen checked into his dorm and went to see the financial advisor about a campus job to help with the cost not covered by his scholarship. The advisor told him the job working in the cafeteria was available, if he wanted it. Allen immediately responded with yes and wanted to know when he would start and what two meals would he work. He was told he'd start on Wednesday after he completed orientation. Allen's puzzled look was noted by the representative who was discussing the job start-up date. Allen was wondering what he was going to do about meals the rest of this day and Tuesday. The advisor assured him he could eat in the cafeteria starting that day and explained once he pulled his course cards, his work schedule would be determined. Relieved, he left the financial office and spent the rest of the morning going over his college catalog to determine what he should take. He learned all the freshmen had to take Orientation to College, a required speech class and English 101. He planned to take Art History, a one level art class, and a two-hour physical education class of his choosing.

His roommate arrived and they spent the afternoon getting acquainted. He said his name was Zack Yancy and he was from Columbus, Ohio. He was going to major in engineering and join his dad's firm when he graduated.

He had attended private schools, graduated from high school the year before, then traveled in Europe the past year.

Allen shared his family had lived in Appalachia for the past few years and he had graduated from high school in May. He was attending college on a partial art scholarship, was going to work in the college cafeteria, was in the National Guard, and worked summers on road construction.

Zack shook his head and asked, "When will you have fun in college?"

Allen replied, "I'm her to get an education. Fun will come later."

Allen pulled his class cards on Tuesday and was scheduled to work in the cafeteria for breakfast from 6:30-8:00 a.m. and would work for the supper meal from 5:30-6:30 p.m.

He telephoned his parents and shared his room assignment, and that he got the cafeteria job. He told his parents working in the cafeteria instead of paying for a meal ticket was saving him $300.00 for the semester. He said his National Guard duty pay, and what he had left of his savings meant he had the difference needed for his second semester. He asked his dad about the tunnel project.

His father shared it was going very slow. Inspectors came often to check air quality. The boring machine ground up rock and then moved out for the men to clear away rubble. Some workers coughed a lot. His dad said he did not. There were days when they had little to do.

Allen asked his dad about the pain in his foot. There as silence for a few minutes before his dad responded. He admitted it bothered him, but he was using the wintergreen alcohol his wife made him take with him as well as a bottle of aspirin. He never stated how bad the pain was. His mother got on the telephone and told him, her pottery and wreaths were sold before she brought more. His allotted time on the phone ended and he hung up.

Allen's roommate, Zack, was not a serious student. He partied most nights rather than studied. Those hours of peace and quiet meant Allen had quality study time. He did watch the college football team practice and went to the college gym for an hour swim twice a week. He didn't have time nor money for dates. He did attend Sunday worship services at the college chapel. The service was very different that the one at home.

He went home for the four-day Thanksgiving break. His mother had prepared a feast and he and his dad ate until they were stuffed. His parents looked older. His mother's hair had gray streaks. The crow's feet around her eyes seemed more pronounced and she had a new set of wrinkles on her forehead. His dad's face was full of pain each time he put that foot down. When he sat in his chair, he removed his boot and elevated the swollen foot.

Allen spent most of his time at home splitting logs and placing them on one end of the porch. He noticed several places that needed chinking and bought the compound to fill in the cracks. His brother, Peter, did not get to come home. He had lunch with Maria's family. Allen told his brother that he needed to talk to him after he returned to college. He couldn't talk in front of his parents.

Once back in school, Allen called his brother and told him about the swelling in his dad's foot and that he was almost dragging that foot. He shared his mother looked very tired. She was spending the weekdays when their dad was in the tunnel site, making wreaths, baskets, and pottery to earn money.

Allen said, "I think mother is trying to make and save as much money as she can in case dad has to quit work."

Peter's Fall Semester

Once Peter aced his first semester in Pre-med. He found anatomy fascinating. The subject matter related to humans, but he could see the relationship to the horses. He checked out a book on horses from the library and did a comparative study of the bones, muscles, and organs of humans and different kinds of horses. In lab, he had to dissect a cat, then identify the bones, muscles and organs.

Maria had taken anatomy several semesters before and they talked about the course. They had little time for each other. Her advance science classes and clinical work at the rural hospital two days a week meant the only time they had together was the nine o'clock nightly date and sitting together at Sunday church service. Some Sundays he had lunch with her family.

During the fall semester, Peter took sixteen hours. He had physiology and the second semester of biochemistry plus his other required classes. Both physiology and biochemistry had three-hour labs each week on Wednesday. He worked on the race horse side of the Cleburne farm from six a.m. to ten a.m. on Tuesday, Thursday and all day on Saturday. He had scheduled all his two hour and four-hour classes in the afternoon. His math class was calculus. He was not prepared for this form of math, and struggled. Having two sciences back-to- back each class day was also a challenge. He even questioned his ability to succeed. Maria had to constantly encourage him. She told him the college also had tutors who could help. Peter met a tutor weekly until he finally understood calculus. He couldn't see how it related to Pre-med.

Jake, Mr. Cleburne's trainer, told Peter that Mr. Cleburne was taking the gray mare to another farm to breed it with another racehorse that had won many races.

Jake said, "Sometimes other racehorses owners bring their horse or horses to Mr. Cleburne's farm for breeding. Cross breeding racehorses make for a faster, stronger racehorse. Owners pay big money to have a racehorse sire another."

That Saturday, Peter learned of artificial insemination as Dr. Nichols took sperm from yet another racehorse to impregnate two horses and impregnate the gray mare. Dr. Nichols told Peter, the next time artificial insemination was needed, he would do it with him telling Peter what to do. During that semester, Dr. Nicholas frequently had Peter observe his work and sometimes walked him through the process. Dr. Nichols kept a log of the hours Peter worked with him to ensure he received credit towards his required one hundred-fifty hours of experience.

Off to the Races

All five of Mr. Cleburne's racehorses were earning money. Some of his horses were two-year-old and one was a year old. His racehorses had great potential for the next racing season. Dr. Nichols and Mr. Cleburne traveled to all the nearby racetracks. During Peter's spring break, he traveled with them. He had never been to a horse race. He knew there were ten to fifteen races in a day at the track. Mr. Cleburne kept a jockey named Nunez on retainer to ride all his horses.

Jake drove the long trailer with the five horses to races nearby. Mr. Cleburne paid the fee for housing the horses and the race entry fee for each horse before they were allowed on the road that led to the stable area. Only those with horses scheduled to race, their trainer, their groomer, owner, and veterinarian were allowed in this area. Local help was on the grounds to clean the stalls when the horses were on the track for their morning exercise. The jockey, whose weight could be no more than one-hundred-ten pounds, used this time on the horse to judge the speed and temperament of each horse. Dr. Nichols checked each horse when it arrived and before each race. Food and water were brought to the horses as they stood in their stall. Peter and Jake talked to other trainers and jockeys. Peter was amazed at the efficiency of back field management. When the call for horses was announced, Peter walked beside Jake as the horse was led to the starting gate and loaded. Mr. Cleburne's one-year-old won by two links and he collected a winning purse. The gray mare came in fourth that day and didn't provide winnings for Cleburne Farm. He had high hopes for three other two-year-old and they didn't disappoint him. His winnings that day were $47,000. The next day, they traveled to Maryland for a Saturday race. Mr. Cleburne had two entries. The two horses had the best chance for continued wins and a chance to win in Lexington's Keenland Park and Louisville's Churchill Downs.

Peter was able to go to one more race that season and was given more responsibilities for the two horses being raced. As he always did, he sang to the horses as he groomed them. He checked them for injury, walked them to the starting gate, and wiped them down after the races. After a race with the horse named Alibi, he mentioned to both Jake and Dr. Nichols, that the horse was favoring its right hind leg. The Cleburne team hearing this, went to check the horse's hind leg. Alibi had a bruise where she had been clipped by another horse during the race.

Peter asked, "What do you do for a horse with a bruise?"

Dr. Nichols said, "You watch it, put an antibiotic cream on it, and rest the horse for a week or two."

Logging in Hours

Once Peter was admitted to Pre-med, he learned how to care for minor injuries to both the racehorses and horses from the farm side of Mr. Cleburne's property. Dr. Nicholas took Peter with him whenever there was an animal on either side of the Cleburne estate that needed care.

Peter had to assist one evening when a cow was in distress while giving birth to a calf. Another time he had to pull the tooth of a cow. He never knew what animal would need special care. Dr. Nichols was giving him experiences he would have on a daily basis when he was a veterinarian. He did the artificial insemination of animals on Mr. Cleburne's estate. He cared for horses with fungus growths. He gave yearly immunization shots to animals. It was also a time for Dr. Nichols to see how good a vet he would become. Mr. Cleburne frequently came to watch as Peter cared for animals. He wanted to make sure he had made the right choice in saying he'd pay for Peter to go to veterinarian school.

Each semester, Peter found how the courses in both biology and chemistry were related. When describing the interconnection to his brother, he said it was like snapping blocks together. He had gotten over his fear of not succeeding. His confidence soared and he was completing his classes with high marks. His final semester, he had two biology classes (bacteriology and genetics) and two chemistry classes (the second semester of organic chemistry and qualitative analysis). Neither genetics nor qualitative analysis had labs.

Maria, his girlfriend, would finish her internship at the rural hospital she had been working two days a week at the ends of the semester and would graduate. Peter planned to ask her to marry him and work at a hospital in Lexington, Kentucky. He wanted to talk to his dad about getting married and he wanted to talk to Maria's father.

The final semester, they seemed to have even less time together. They could only manage one or two nightly nine o'clock dates a week. Most Sundays, he attended church services with her family and ate at the Nichol's home, but they were never alone.

Peter Is Not Accepted

Peter took six hours during the summer session of his senior year. He found each science class built on what he'd had the semester before. He would take his last nine hours of Pre-med in the fall of 1953 and then immediately applied for veterinarian school.

The University of Kentucky looked at Peter's grade point average. He had a 3.1 average. The college required a 3.0 average. Dr. Nichol's log of Peter's one hundred-fifty hours of work with the racehorses was not accepted. The board of the School of Veterinarian Medicine required one-hundred-fifty hours working with all kinds and sizes of animals He needed to work for an animal clinic. He had to have exposure to all kinds of animals and their needs, not just racehorses.

After he graduated from Blyne College in January 1954, Peter went to work for Storrington Animal Hospital in East Ridge, Kentucky which was located about ten miles north of Blyne. He did everything from stitching wounds, cleaning out infected area, giving inoculations, pulling teeth, and assisting in surgery.

Peter worked three-ten-hour-shifts a week at the animal hospital and three-ten-hour shifts for Mr. Cleburne. On Sunday, he went to church and had lunch with Maria's family. Some Sundays, Maria had to work at the hospital in Cincinnati as part of her internship. Maria had graduated in June, 1953, and had to do the one-year internship before she could take her state boards and be licensed. On occasion, he would drive to Cincinnati on Saturday evening to be with her. He'd stay at Allen's place. Peter wanted to marry her after she finished that year. He reasoned she could work at a hospital in Lexington while he attended veterinary school. She told him she wanted to spend an additional year working as a surgical nurse. She wanted to wait.

This exasperated Peter. He reasoned they had been dating for five years. He wanted more than a girlfriend. He wanted a wife. She was just as adamant that she should have the opportunity to specialize in surgical nursing.

On a four-day weekend, Peter went home. He wanted to talk to his dad about marriage. He wanted to give her the ring he bought for her birthday.

His dad advised him to talk to her more about marriage, but not pin her down to a date. His dad said, "Making demands was not the way to start a marriage. Look at the responsibilities you would place on her. She'd be the 'bread winner' and you the student trapsing off to school each day."

"Marriage is a lifetime commitment. It is not a fifty/fifty arrangement. It is the giving of yourself one hundred percent of the time. Marriage is a blending of two personalities. Each of you have strong values and are of the same faith. Those are two strong traits in a marriage. You need to respect each other, listen to each other's needs, and love each other unconditionally. God should be centered to your marriage. Think before you speak. It will save a lot of headaches. You need to talk about having children and how you plan to raise them."

"Finances need to be understood, and you both need to be watchful of spending. You know what overspending caused in our lives. Avoid that. Society has changed since your mother and I married. It is a modern world, and not all women want or can afford to stay home. Children may go to day care. Husbands have to take some household responsibilities and help with cleaning or cooking. Both of you need to know about income, expenses and saving. Care of the children is as much your responsibility as it would be for Maria. You need to communicate. Think about how you can relate to each other, then ask yourself, are you ready for marriage? Are you ready to have a family? Are you ready to live together for the rest of your lives?"

"Through the years of your mother and my marriage, my demands and stubbornness has caused unnecessary problems. Don't demand, work together in all things of importance. It makes for a more peaceful and happy marriage."

"One day, as you work with Dr. Nichols, consider talking to him about his view of marriage.

It will reflect Maria's concept of what it is supposed to be. Have faith that God will be a part of your marriage. Turn to Him in daily prayer and in time of need."

Flora called her men in for supper. Tom and his son turned toward the cabin and began to walk in that direction.

As they walked, Peter turned toward his dad and said, 'Dad, you have given me a lot to think about. Maybe I should wait until next Christmas to give Maria a ring. We have a lot to discuss before we say, I Do."

Life Off Campus

Allen only lived on campus his freshman year. He rented a space at Mrs. Weaver's home which was just a few blocks from campus. Mrs. Weaver asked for twenty dollars rent per month plus upkeep of her yard. He had a bedroom, kitchenet, bathroom and a small setting area with a futon sofa and coffee table. It had at one time been a part of her living space, but age, health and loneliness had her reorganize her living space and created the apartment Allen rented. The whole house had forced gas heat and carpeted floors which meant it would be warm during the winter.

He applied for a summer job cleaning the office of the Jacobson Architect Firm and doing small tasks as asked during his nightly two hours of work. The pay was thirty dollars/month.

Allen's summer job at Jacobson Architect Firm, his National Guard duty pay and summer training pay as well as his partial scholarship, provided enough money to complete his second year of college. He continued cleaning the architect firm's offices during the school year. Monthly, he received twenty-five dollars for National Guard duty. He had fifty-five dollars per month to live on and money left over to save toward his junior year of college.

He continued to rent from Mrs. Weaver in exchange for him doing yard work and other small jobs for her throughout his college studies. Allen had enough money to pay his rent. His mother gave him fruits and vegetables she had canned, and preserves she made. Mrs. Weaver always gave him a half loaf of bread she'd made each week. He budgeted himself five dollars per week for purchased groceries and gas, if needed. Unless the weather was severe, he walked everywhere. He always had a little money left over at the end of the month. He wondered if the money saved each month and National Guard summer maneuvers' income would be enough for his junior year of college. He looked at all his income and his expenses and felt his tension melt away.

Working for the architect firm made Allen aware of another career possibility. As he perceived it, geometric designs were another form of art. He thought about the college financial advisor's comment on co-oping. There wasn't an art co-op program, but if he changed his major to architecture, he could possibly co-op with the Jacobson Firm.

He'd work one semester and attend classes one semester. It would take him at least one extra year to graduate, but he'd have no debt. He made an appointment with the college financial advisor. He asked the advisor if he would lose his scholarship if he changed his major to architecture and his minor to art? Initially, she said yes. She thought about the request and asked how many hours in his current major of art had he completed? Allen replied he had completed eighteen hours of art classes.

The advisor looked off as she considered options. She stood and told Allen she needed to check with the financial administrator. No student had ever asked to continue receiving their award and reversing the reason for the award from one field of study to another.

The advisor said, she'd be back in a few minutes. She took his academic folder with her to her boss. From the chair where Allen was seated, he could see her knock on her boss' door, then go inside.

The minutes ticked away. Allen stood and walked around the room. He read captions under pictures hanging on the wall. He looked at the books on her book shelves. He read her credentials on certificates on the wall behind her desk. He kept watching the clock, 10, 20, 28 minutes ticked off before she came out of her boss' office. Allen sat back down. The advisor told him, if he continued taking one three-hour art class each semester or more as a co-op student, he would have thirty hours of art to graduate and at least thirty hours in architecture or a second major, and he could keep his scholarship. She said the second problem would be to find a firm that would agree to a co-op student. If a firm was found, he'd have to take classes the first semester of his junior year and co-op the second semester.

Allen stated he'd worked for the Jacobson Firm during the summer between his freshman and sophomore years of college and had a daily two-hour cleaning job with them during his sophomore school year. The advisor made a note of his current employment with them. She said she would contact that company and see if the firm would accept him as a co-op student. He left her office hopeful that the Jacobson Firm would accept him as a co-op student.

He heard nothing for four weeks before he received a letter of acceptance. It stated he would attend classes during the fall and work for them during the spring semester. He would be required to do a three-year co-op. He was employed as summer help as he had done the year before. He telephoned his parents and his brother to share his good news.

In early August, Hurricane Elsa came up the east coast as a Category Two hurricane and caused extensive flooding. The governor of South Carolina requested guardsmen to help with rescue efforts and clean-up. His unit was deplored and stayed for six weeks. He missed the first two weeks of class and had to play catch-up in his Geometric Design art class, Basic Architect Design, A History of Architecture, a math class, and two electives.

Mr. Jacobson took time to go over basic information about architecture, He told Allen there were three various types of architecture: technical, solutions, and enterprise architects. Each has a function on any architectural project. He continued and explained each type. An enterprise architect works with the individual or company on a design project. He discusses with the client the building design and landscape for the structure which determines the job of the solutions architect who creates all the drawings necessary for the project to be constructed. The technical architect works out the fine details. Allen was assigned to work for a period of time with each kind of architect. He learned the steps taken to plan, execute and complete each project. He had to do some drawings, list the steps on how to design the structure and why, and create the drawings to show the process from beginning to completion. He was paid three hundred dollars a month during his work semester. This was more than enough to pay for his schooling and money was left over. Each semester, he put three hundred dollars in his savings account.

Living at Mrs. Weaver's for twenty dollars a month, gas at twenty-three cents a gallon, grocery needs at twenty-five dollars a month, and twenty dollars a month for several dates to the movies, took away his worry of whether he'd have enough money to complete his education.

During the winter of his junior year of college, the weather was brutal. Heavy snows, fierce winds, ice and a month with below zero temperatures kept Mrs. Weaver indoors. Each week she gave Allen a grocery list and money to cover the cost. If she needed him for any reason, she would knock on the kitchen wall and he'd go over to her side of the duplex to check on her.

The house was old and not well insulated. He bought a roll of heavy plastic and tacked the plastic over the windows. Both sides of the duplex were ten degrees warmer. He wrapped the water pipes so they would not freeze. Every time he saw Mrs. Weaver, she appeared weaker than the time before. Whenever he asked her if she was alright, she always replied that she was just tired of being cooped up in the house.

The week before Christmas there was a break in the weather. Mrs. Weaver's daughter drove to her mother's house with food, cough syrup ,and a small artificial tree. She was going to stay through the Christmas week. Allen had wondered if he could leave her and check on his own parents. Thankfully he was able to visit for a week with his parents. He and Peter had been very worried how their parents had coped with the severe cold.

A Bitter Cold Christmas and Following Months

The snow and subzero weather before Christmas improved. It was still very cold, but tolerable when Allen was at the cabin. Peter, likewise, made plans to be home for Christmas. The brothers talked with their parents on the telephone once a week. Neither felt their parents sounded like themselves on the telephone. They questioned if it was the harsh weather was the reason their dad had not working for over a month, or something else?

Allen had driven home on Wednesday before Christmas. Peter would get off on Saturday afternoon. Allen noticed the wood pile he had stacked on the porch on his last trip home was nearly gone. Chicken droppings had not been picked up. His mother, who usually had baked goods made and the room decorated, had done neither. His dad stayed in his chair by the fireplace most of the time with his foot elevated. He called Peter and described the cabin and the worn looks of their parents. Peter asked off and left on Thursday instead of Saturday as he had originally planned.

Peter and Allen both noticed how their parents had aged in the past few months. Neither moved as quickly as they used to move. Both had stress written all over their faces. They had deep creases on their foreheads and a pinched look from concern for Tom's health and worry about his ability to return to work when the bitter cold ended.

The brothers chinked between the cabin logs, cut firewood and stacked it on the porch, cleaned the chicken house and yard, and hunted one day for wild game. Peter sat down with his mother and made a grocery list and went shopping for her. She appreciated that she did not have to go out into the cold.

Allen made a pot of soup and a pan of cornbread for supper as his mother laid down on the couch with the old quilt over her. While his parents napped, he straightened up the house, and baked a pan of sugar cookies. He took the Christmas wreath his mother had made many years before and hung it over the fireplace. He looked in her craft room. It had few items on the shelves and the room was very chilly. He and Peter tacked the sheets of plastic over the windows from the inside to block some of the draft.

Once the groceries were put up and the food was ready, Peter gently shook his mother and told her supper was ready. His dad stirred and started to get up. He winched when he put his bad foot on the ground and limped to the table.

Peter asked his dad about his foot after supper as he returned to his chair by the fireplace and raised his foot to the foot stool. He asked, had he twisted it?

His dad said, "No, it was the weather that caused it to hurt."

Peter was not convinced and asked to look at the foot. He removed the boot and elastic bandage his dad had on his ankle. He asked his dad to move his foot up and down. His dad could not move it. Peter gently pressed on the ankle and Peter could see the swelling. Flora and Allen had sat near Tom as Peter examined the foot. It was evident he needed to see a doctor. Peter suggested they drive to the rural hospital nearby and have it x-rayed. For once, he did not protest.

The emergency room doctor ordered x-rays. The doctor told Tom and his family that he needed to see a doctor who specialized in orthopedic surgery.

Tom protested. He said, "We don't have the money to go to Cincinnati and have someone operate on my foot. Where would we stay? Who'd take care of the chickens? How would my wife do her crafts, if we are in Cincinnati?"

He had every excuse he could think of to prevent having to go to Cincinnati. The doctor told him, if he didn't do something, he would lose his foot and possibly his leg. Tom said nothing. He looked at the doctor, his wife and his sons and then said it is time to go home.

Allen and Peter stayed up late and talked. They determined it would be better if their parents could stay with Allen in Cincinnati. At breakfast the next morning, the brothers brought up the subject of their parents staying at Allen's place in Cincinnati. He would sleep on the futon and their parents could sleep in his double bed.

Peter spoke up. He said, "Allen and I are both working and have money in savings. We can cover the cost of your medical needs, dad."

Again, their dad asked, "What about the chickens?"

Peter replied, "John and Ida Mae Avery have six children. Give the chickens to them. They can use the eggs and chickens."

The Avery family, members of their church with a large family to support, were thankful for the offer of the chickens and few winter vegetables still in the ground. That family had little, but were very generous with their time to help others. Now was an opportunity to help them.

Sunday morning Peter left for Blyne and his parents rode with Allen to Cincinnati. They would make an appointment with the specialist the emergency room doctor had recommended. It took several weeks to get an appointment. After the initial visit, x-rays were taken and compared with the ones previously taken. The ankle was still badly swollen and the skin showed signs of discoloration. Medicine was prescribed to ease the pain and another pill was given to reduce the swelling. A brace was made to hold the foot in place until surgery could be scheduled. The surgeon told them there was only a fifty-fifty chance that surgery would resolve the problem. The brace was temporary. The discoloration indicated there was little circulation to the foot and could be a warning sign of Tom losing the foot, if nothing was done.

In February, surgery was done. Tom wore a cast, used crutches, then had physical therapy. In July, Allen took his parents' home. Peter had requested time to get the cabin ready and plant a late garden. He bought a dozen chicks and cleaned the chicken yard. There were many young saplings that he cut down and cut into firewood for the next winter. Peter replenished his mother's kitchen with food easy to prepare and even bought a few canned meats, fruits, and vegetables that normally his mother would have grown and canned herself.

Tom tried to get on his tractor, but when he put one foot on the tractor, the weight on the braced foot was so great, he cried out in pain. He slammed his hands across the steering wheel and just cried. There was one more thing he could no longer do. He felt he was a useless man. He could no longer hold a job and now he could no longer work his land. He promised himself many years before that he would never be in a predicament where he could not provide for his family, and now he was dependent on his sons instead of the other way around. Flora called her sons and told them of their dad's depression. Both came home that weekend and alternated coming every other weekend after that.

In late September, when Peter was home for the weekend, he saw his dad's foot without a sock. Pus oozed out of a sore by the surgical scare. He took his dad and his momma to the rural hospital. Tom was in pain and hoped for something to ease the pain. Upon examining the foot, the doctor noticed the red streak of gangrene going up the leg. The rural doctor called a surgeon in Cincinnati and told him Tom had gangrene and was on his way to the hospital. Allen was called and met them at the hospital.

Tom was very angry and depressed about the emergency need to amputate his foot and possibly part of his leg. Though in extreme pain he grumbled as Peter drove them to the hospital.

In slurred speech, he asked, "Why now when our boys are grown and you and I could relax, do our crafts, and enjoy the peacefulness of the mountain? I won't be able to work and again we will have to struggle to survive. I can't do that to you, Flora. Peter, turn around and take me home. I'd rather die there than in a hospital."

Peter had his lights and flashers on and was speeding at fifty miles an hour. The medicine given in the emergency room made Tom drowsy and he slept the rest of the way to the hospital. He was taken from the car into surgery Allen met them at the emergency room. He hugged his mother who had tears streaming down her cheeks and told her and his brother, Peter, he would go to the business office and began filling out the paperwork. Peter and his mother went to the surgical waiting room.

Flora had a silent conversation with God. "Lord, my husband needs your help once again. His foot, injured when Peter was a baby, has gangrene and the infection is in the bone of his leg. He is in the operating room right now and doctors are cutting off his foot and maybe part of his leg as you are aware. Please, I beg you, answer my prayer and let him get well. He is so depressed that he won't be able to walk again and will be confined to a wheelchair. Through my prayers, dear God, show me the way to help my husband."

Several hours passed with no word of Tom's condition. Flora tightly griped the arms of the chair until her knuckles were white. It was 1 A.M. when the surgeon came out of the surgical unit and knelt in front of Flora. Allen and Peter sat in the chairs beside their mother as the surgeon explained the foot and up to the knee was amputated because the infection had spread in the foot and leg bone. He assured her Tom would recover, but it was going to take a lot of time and therapy. Flora burst into tears and her whole body was trembling. Her sons each reached for her and held on to her until she could compose herself. Though she could not see Tom until much later that day, she refused to leave the surgical waiting room. Coffee was brought out to the family and a pillow and heated blanket was given to Flora.

Tom was hospitalized for several weeks then moved to rehab on another floor for another month. Flora rode the bus each day to the hospital to observe and be instructed on how to help him. After he was released, he had to go back to the hospital for therapy. Flora, Peter and Allen went to the orthotics lab the day Tom was fitted with the artificial leg. He was uncertain about wearing it and grumbled.

Peter hadn't been accepted in veterinary school yet and came to Cincinnati every weekend. He had time with Maria and time to whittle with his dad. The diversion lifted his dad's spirits, if only for a little while. Allen's half of the duplex was very small and when Peter visited, he slept in a sleeping bag on the carpeted floor. His parents continued to live with Allen in the duplex for nine more months while adjustments to the fit of the artificial limb were made.

Nearly a year later, Tom and Flora went home, hopefully to have a normal life Peter and Allen knew their parents would need help after they returned to the cabin and alternated weekends to spend a part or whole day at the cabin doing the things their parents could no longer do for themselves. Each week the brothers noticed the decline. Tom and Flora were thankful their sons came and made it easier for them to stay in their cabin.

The winter of 1954 saw a strong unknown strand of the flu across the United States and Europe. Many died of the flu. The elderly people were especially hard hit in Appalachia. Tom was one of the people who caught the flu, lingered for a few weeks with a high fever, congestion and fatigue. He did not respond to the medicine prescribed and died with Flora sitting beside him. She called her sons and they came home. Tom was buried in the church cemetery behind the little white church where they attended.

After Tom Cole's death, his wife remained in her Appalachian cabin through the rest of that winter. The bitter cold and above average snow had her struggling to keep her chickens alive, difficulty getting her crafts to market, or to even get her firewood from the porch to the fireplace inside her cabin. Neither Peter nor Allen could travel on the impassible roads to check on their mother. Even the telephone line was knocked down by the weight of the snow and ice.

Peter and Allen talked on the telephone daily. They had to do something. Their mother could not stay in the cabin alone. Peter was traveling a lot during race season with Dr. Nichols. Moving his mother to Blyne wouldn't work. He lived in a studio apartment above the horses in one of the stables. Allen told his brother, he could afford to move into a larger place, so there would be room for his mother.

Allen weekly bought the Sunday paper and looked in the classified section for rental houses. He found a two-bedroom duplex on Evergreen Street and a three-bedroom house on Hill Street with a screened porch for rent or for sale. Rent was fifty dollars per month or fifty-seven dollars per month house note, if purchased. It he bought the three-bedroom house, his mother would have a room for her crafts. He told his mother of the house for sale and said he was going to buy it. She'd have an area for crafts and, a home with her son who could care for her. His momma was resistant to the move. The cabin, her church friends, and her next-door neighbor, Emmy, lived in Appalachia. They were her life. Other than her sons, she knew no one in Cincinnati. She didn't want the faster pace of life. She had all kinds of excuses why she couldn't move in with her son.

Mrs. Weaver moved in with her daughter after she caught the flu the past winter. No one was living in her half of the duplex. On one of her visits to her home, Allen shared with Mrs. Weaver, his landlord, that he was looking for a larger place to live. He was moving his mother in with him. He told her of the house on Hill Street for sale and was considering buying it. He was in his fourth year of college and had savings. He had rented from Mrs. Weaver for three years and maintained her property during that time.

Mts. Weaver told her daughter to offer her six-room house to Allen. Her daughter asked at what price and how much did she want as a down payment?

Mrs. Weaver shook her head. " I don't want him to finance it through the bank. He can continue to pay me. Offer the house for sixty-five hundred with no down payment. He is still in college."

She had her daughter drive over to her property. She knocked on Allen's door and he answered. He invited Mrs. Weaver and her daughter to sit down.

Mrs. Weaver inquired, "Have you purchased the house on Hill Street you told me about on my last visit?"

Allen said, "I've found a house, but must see about financing it."

Mrs. Weaver smiled, and asked, "Allen, would you like to buy this house for six thousand five hundred dollars? I don't want you to finance through the bank and pay all that interest. You can continue to pay me. The only money you would have to put down is one dollar to record the sale and transfer of deed."

Allen couldn't believe what he was hearing. He asked, "What would the house payments be?"

She asked, "Can you afford fifty-five dollars a month."

He gave an enthusiastic, "YES!".

Mrs. Weaver had an attorney write up a deed and the terms of the transaction. Allen signed after Mrs. Weaver signed the deed. Allen handed the attorney the one dollar and handed Mrs. Weaver the $55.00 house note.

That weekend he began removing the wall between the two kitchens. His brother, Peter, was in Cincinnati that weekend to visit his girlfriend, Maria, and helped with the removal. He began sketching possible changes to the house. As a senior project in architecture, Allen

had to design a house or building, make the initial drawings, (Expertise Architecture), work out all the details to accomplish his structure, including landscaping (solution Architecture), then do all the technical aspects for completion (Technical Architecture). He decided to use his new home. He did the series of drawings of the inside and outside of the house, the exterior, and the landscaping. He had to price materials, determine how much of each was needed, and had to have it approved for the architect license upon acceptance of the project and graduation. Mr. Jacobson, his co-op boss and mentor, questioned him on each phase and how his plan could be more effective.

Peter's Acceptance

Peter was finally accepted at the University of Kentucky School of Veterinary Medicine. Dr. Nichols, the Cleburne veterinarian, knew several of the professors there and told Peter they would go to Georgetown together. As they traveled, the conversation was about the description of the school program and the kind of work schedule Peter could have.

There was a period of silence as Dr. Nichols maneuvered through the morning traffic, then Dr. Nichols began to talk about his family, and in particular, his daughter, Maria. He told Peter she always wanted to be a nurse. As a child, she'd play nurse and would wear an old stethoscope of his around her neck. She would listen for the heartbeat of her younger sisters and even the animals. He thought she might follow in his footsteps and become a veterinarian.

Her dad shifted the conversation from Maria's passion for nursing to Peter's intentions. It surprised Peter that her dad was so bold with his questioning.

Peter told Dr. Nichols, "I love Maria and intended to ask her to marry me now that I will be in veterinary school. She could work in Lexington and we could rent an apartment near the agricultural center. Peter said the course of study for vet school took ten semesters without a summer break. If we aren't married and she is in Cincinnati and I am in Lexington, we will rarely see each other. I have bought a ring and plan to give it to her at Christmas."

Her dad looked at Peter and asked, "Have you thought of all the responsibilities of marriage?"

Peter replied, "This past fall, I had a long talk with my dad about marriage. He shared marriage is the blending of two personalities, financial obligations, and children. He emphasized marriage wasn't a fifty-fifty proposition. It is the give-of- self one hundred percent."

Peter continued, "I've thought about his words a lot and that is why I've waited until I was accepted in veterinary school. I'm asking for your permission to marry Maria. Will you give us your blessing?"

"Peter, yes, I approve and give my blessings. Give her your ring at Christmas as you have planned. I ask you to wait until she finishes this internship first. I feel she needs to finish her dream first, so there are no regrets later on that interferes with your relationship. She finishes in June of next year."

The white fences of the college came into view and the conversation shifted again. This time to the enormity of the grounds, the animal hospital, silos, barns, many other buildings and students in their gray scrubs.

Proposal

Peter's first semester at the University of Kentucky was filled with long hours in class and work in the animal hospital. He had little time to think about anything else. His weekend visit in Cincinnati to see Maria were rare. They talked on the telephone twice a week, but their schedules allowed for little else.

He thought about Dr. Nichols' advice, 'Give Maria time to finish her dream. She finishes her internship in June. June seemed like a short period of time then, but now, as he lived through each day of the separation, it felt like an eternity. Peter finished his first semester and had a break for Christmas. He went to Cincinnati and stayed at Allen's place.

Maria worked Christmas Eve and Peter decided to take her to a nice restaurant for Christmas lunch. He'd ask her then to marry him. He'd read that the Ohioan Hotel and Resort was serving a special Christmas lunch complete with champagne, a rose for each lady and music for dancing. He thought it would be the perfect place to ask her for her hand in marriage. He made reservations. He spent extra time with his dressing for lunch and even bought her a bouquet of mixed flowers. He put a splash of cologne on his face, put on his sport jacket and put the ring case in his pocket.

Maria was dressed in a red wool dress with a matching red coat. He could not take his eyes off of her. They were seated with a view of the Ohio River as he had requested. Soft Christmas music played as they ate their meal. Jazz was played as couples twirled around on the dance floor. Peter couldn't have asked for a more perfect setting for his proposal. A chocolate liqueur infused pear and coffee were served for dessert. As she picked up her fork to take a bite of the pear, Peter took out the ring case and opened it. He softly spoke her name and she looked up to see the diamond ring in Peter's hand as he asked, "Maria, will you marry me?"

Maria said nothing. She held the fork with pear in one hand and put her other hand over her mouth. Tears slide down her cheeks. Peter thought she was so overwhelmed. He had no idea she was about to tell him, no. Silence followed. Peter closed the ring case and put it back in his pocket. He turned and faced the water as Maria got up and left the table.

Peter paid the bill and left. He didn't follow her. He walked along the river walk and tried to understand.

That evening Maria called Peter at Allen's duplex and asked if he'd come over. He deserved an explanation. Peter knocked on her apartment door and said her name as he walked into her living room. He did not kiss her as he always did when they greeted. He sat in the barrel chair and faced her as she sat on the sofa. He said nothing.

Maria tried to explain her reason for not accepting his ring. She said, "Peter, I do love you and at some time in the future, I want to become your wife. YOU HAVE TWO AND A HALF YEARS OF SCHOOLING IN Georgetown. If I continue at the hospital during those two years, I can become the head surgical nurse at my job in Cincinnati. It has always been my dream. We have loved each other through five years, and I don't believe that will ever change whether we marry tomorrow or two years from now. I'm not saying no, I'm saying give me more time."

Peter was both hurt and angry and felt it was better to say nothing at all. He got up, said, "Goodnight, Maria" and left.

A Change of Heart

Maria told her parents of the Christmas fiasco. They were shocked. Her dad shared that Peter and he had talked, and he'd given his blessings to their marriage.

Her dad continued, "Your mother and I expected to hear he gave you the ring he'd bought and you'd set a summer date. Maria, he has allowed you to finish your dream. You have gone together for five years. He is deeply in love with you. Do you feel the same way about Peter?"

"Yes, I love him with all my heart." Maria was crying.

"Maria, when do you have two days off?"

"I am off Wednesday and Thursday. Why?"

"There is a new full-service, modern hospital that has opened in the last couple of months on the western tip of Lexington and about four miles from the veterinary school. I'd like to take you there Wednesday. Let you see the hospital, talk to the nursing director and tour the facility. Are you willing to go see it and talk to the nursing director?"

"What time will you pick me up?" Maria asked.

Wednesday, Maria and her dad went to Lexington. The nursing director met Maria and her dad, then took Maria on a tour of the hospital. From the glassed area above surgery, Maria could see the modern equipment. It was very much like the surgical department where she was working. After walking through the hospital, they went back to the nursing administrator's office. For over an hour, Maria asked questions and was pleased with the responses she heard. She was offered a surgical nurse position to begin when she finished her internship in June.

"Dad, how can I erase the pain I've caused Peter?"

"MARIA, YOU CAN'T CHANGE THE PAST. You can share what you learned today and ask him if he would marry you in June?"

Maria gave her dad a kiss and thanked him for bringing her to visit the hospital. She added and thank you for making me aware of my inconsiderate behavior.

Maria called Peter that evening. He heard the telephone ring, but ignored it at first. On the seventh ring, he picked up. Maria told him of her trip to Lexington, the tour of the hospital, and the job offer to begin in June after she had finished her training in Cincinnati. Peter was about to respond when she asked, "Peter, will you marry me in June?"

Peter shouted, "YES."

They talked for another fifteen minutes making plans to find a place to live and where to have the wedding. Because of Flora Cole's health and the fact that Maria was living in Cincinnati, they decided to get married there.

Allen's Senior Project

Allen spent his senior year in college completing his design project on his home. He spent several months drawing the plans. The two-bedroom duplex would be converted to a three- bedroom home with an open floor plan of living room, dining area, and kitchen. The former kitchen in the apartment became a craft room with a wall of shelves, a large counter for clay and some tools. The drawers underneath the counter would house Flora's paints, brushes, dried bagged flowers, ribbons and sewing materials.

Allen had designed an upstairs with two bedrooms, a small lounge area and storage. The hall bathroom was not changed. The downstairs bedroom was enlarged. The bathroom and closet were enlarged. The remainder of that room was added to the craft room. Outside, Allen created a courtyard with a half wall brick enclosure. Flower boxes were made to sit on top of the brick walls. Allen intended to ask his mother to plant the flower bulbs in each. He added a carport with an archway-opening on to the covered porch.

In phase two, he planned to add a screened porch off the back of the house. All windows would be changed to triple pane with argon gas between layers of glass. He removed all the old shrubs and added low growth evergreens. Three Japanese red maples were planted in the front yard. The two previous windows in the front room were replaced with a larger single window. A flagstone walkway was added from the driveway to the courtyard.

His mother watched as he made all the changes with her approval of the space he was creating. He asked his momma about colors to paint the rooms and carpet to be laid on the floors. In every way, he was trying to make it a home she'd want to live in with him. His asking of her suggestions was working. She was taking ownership of this space.

In early spring, she asked her sons to plant her summer garden at the cabin. They questioned her request. They thought they had convinced her to move permanently to Cincinnati. They plowed the garden, and she planted the seeds. She watched as the sprouts began to push their heads up through the soft ground. Each day she walked her garden, bent down and pulled weeds, and felt the pains of stooping. She had to admit it. She could no longer tend her garden, nor can the vegetables, nor make the preserves as she had done for so many years.

One Saturday night, when both sons were having supper with her at the cabin, she told them, it was time for her to move to Cincinnati and Allen's house.

A week later, her sons returned with a U-Haul truck. Flora went from room to room. She ran her hand across the sofa with the quilt her mother-in-law made for them as a wedding present. She folded it and held it up to her chest. She wrapped the good dishes she'd had since her wedding and had her sons put them in the truck. The empty buffet her father had made was covered with a quilt and placed on the truck. Clothes were packed. Craft supplies, her potter's wheel, tools, and walking sticks Tom had whittled were placed on the floor of the truck.

Her sons loaded her washing machine and left the wringer washer in the shed for someone else to use. She told them she'd be back. She went to the church cemetery and sat by Tom's grave for a few minutes and said a silent prayer. The minister seeing her there walked out toward her. She stood and walked toward him. She told him she was moving to Cincinnati and would not be coming back. He asked about her land and the cabin. She took the keys to Peter's old truck and handed them to the minister. She said, "Last Sunday at church, you said the Avery place had burned down and the family of eight have been parceled out to the neighbors. I want to give my land and cabin to the Avery family. My cabin has most of its furniture, chickens, and a garden planted. Don't let the kudzu devour the cabin. Give new life to the Avery family. I won't be coming back.

She got in her car and drove back to the cabin. Her sons had the U-Haul packed with the belongings she intended to keep. Peter pulled out of the dirt driveway first, followed by Allen and his mother. Tears clouded her vision as they left the dirt driveway for their journey to her new life with Allen in Cincinnati. Another chapter of their lives had ended.

Author Josephine Graven

Josephine Graven, known to most as Jo, is a widow with four adult children, six adult grandchildren and four very young, great-grandchildren. Jo has had four careers during her seventy-nine years of life. She was a medical technician for eight years, an educator for thirty-two years, a storyteller for over forty years, and now is a writer with three published books, **Perseverance Road** published in 2021, **A Collection of Short Stories as Written by the Energized Turtle** published in 2021, and now the sequel to **Perseverance Road** titled **Life's Winding Road.**

Josephine has been an active member of Delta Kappa Gama International Educators Society for thirty years and continues to serve as needed.

Jo spends much of her free time socializing with friends, playing cards with friends, and playing board games with family. She spends many hours writing and dallying in different paint mediums, though just an untrained artist. Josephine enjoys listening to classical music and loves to sing along with songs of the fifties, sixties and some seventies tunes.

Made in the USA
Columbia, SC
09 January 2025

51575239R00052